For Melissa

Editorial Director, James Kuse

Managing Editor, Ralph Luedtke

Production Editor/Manager, Richard Lawson

Photographic Editor, Gerald Koser

Copy Editor, Norma Barnes

Associate Editor, Beverly Wiersum Charette

ISBN 0-89542-934-9 195

The Great Piggy Bank Robbery

Written and Illustrated by

Russ Biernat

There once was a turtle named Albert. He lived in Mudville, a sleepy little town near the Mucky Wump River. Albert's only ambition in life was to become a sheriff.

But, in Mudville, there was never any need for a sheriff. Everyone was friendly and peaceful. The only time the townspeople ever used the jail was for ice cream socials.

So Albert would go off by himself to sit by the riverbank and dream and dream and dream.

One day Albert was eating a peanut butter and jelly sandwich under his favorite tree. Suddenly he heard a voice say, "Hello."

Turning around, Albert saw a strange-looking creature standing up out of the water. It had two big ears and a very long nose. "My goodness," said Albert with astonishment. "Who are you?"

"Proboscis P. Pachyderm's the name, but my friends call me Packy," said the elephant.

It wasn't long before Albert and Packy became good friends. Both of them liked to play games. Sometimes they played cowboys and Indians. Of course, Albert's favorite game was sheriff and robber.

But Albert soon became weary of all these make-believe games. He wanted to be a real sheriff chasing real robbers.

Early one morning, two strangers named Alfonso and Bonzo rode into town seeking both fame and fortune. They proceeded directly to the Mudville Bank.

"Nobody move. This is a holdup!" Bonzo
said with a grin as he entered the bank.
Nobody moved, not even a mouse.

"Outrageous, simply outrageous. You'll never get away with this," blustered Mr. Quigley, the bank president. Alfonso tied him up tightly with his best bank robber knot.

But get away they did. Somehow Alfonso and Bonzo managed to push the big piggy bank through the front door of the bank and down Main Street. Then they silently slipped out of town without anyone noticing.

Meanwhile, Mr. Quigley loosened the rope just enough to untie himself. Huffing and puffing, he ran toward the mayor's office. He was shouting, "My bank's been robbed! My bank's been robbed!"

By this time, the whole town knew the bank had been robbed. But what could the mayor do?

"I'm helpless," he cried. "Mudville doesn't have a sheriff."

When he heard the mayor, Albert saw his chance to become a real sheriff.

Mr. Quigley was about ready to give up. His piggy bank was lost forever. Then Albert, in a small voice, said with determination, "I'll be sheriff!"

The mayor and Mr. Quigley huddled in a quickly assembled meeting, and the decision was unanimous.

"Congratulations! You're the sheriff of Mudville," His Honor, the Mayor, proclaimed after he handed Albert his star.

Albert already had his own gun. "But I'll need someone to help me track down the bank robbers," said Albert to the mayor. "Packy's got a good nose for following trails. He can be my deputy and scout." Everyone agreed.

Jumping on his horse, Albert was off to chase the bank robbers.

Of course Alfonso, Bonzo and the piggy bank were by this time miles away from Mudville. But their getaway wasn't going exactly the way they had planned it. Pushing a fat piggy bank **up** Old Pogie Mountain wasn't easy.

Both were sure they had made off with the loot until they looked back down the road toward Mudville and saw Albert and Packy. "Oh! Oh!" cried Alfonso. "It looks like a posse coming after us."

Lickety-split, Alfonso and Bonzo headed down the back side of the mountain.

But no matter how fast they traveled, they just weren't fast enough to get away from Sheriff Albert and Deputy Packy. You see, Albert knew about a shortcut around Old Pogie Mountain. He, and Packy were waiting for the robbers at the bottom of the mountain.

"I have an idea," Albert said to Packy. "You climb a tree, and when they are underneath, jump down and capture the alligator. I'll take care of the bear."

Packy liked to climb trees. So he quickly climbed up the tree without being noticed.

"I think we lost them," Alfonso said with a chuckle to Bonzo. Just as he said that. . . .

. . . Packy jumped out of his tree, did a double
somersault in midair, and landed on top of Alfonso
with a loud—**KBOOM**.

When Bonzo looked back to see what all the
commotion was about, there was Albert behind
him. "You're under arrest," Albert said. "Put your
hands up or I'll tickle your belly button and then
have Packy sit on top of you."

Well, Bonzo didn't like having his belly button tickled, and he certainly didn't want Packy to sit on top of him. He could see what had happened to his pal, Alfonso. So he raised his hands and surrendered peacefully to Albert.

When they brought the bank robbers back to town, Albert and Packy were given a hero's welcome by the citizens of Mudville. The mayor and Mr. Quigley decided to erect a statue honoring them for saving Mudville's piggy bank.

Everyone was happy—everyone, that is, except Alfonso and Bonzo. But they did get free food and lodging in the town jail for several years.

By the end of that day, Albert was exhausted. After hanging up his gun and cowboy hat, he slipped out of his turtle shell, put on his pajamas, brushed his teeth and went to bed. He quickly fell asleep.

Packy slept in his favorite tree.

Everyone in town spread the news about Albert the Sheriff and his deputy, Packy. To this day no one has ever seen another bank robber in Mudville.

New titles in the *Good Friends* series:

Alex in Wonderland
Big Blue Marble
Dugan the Duck
Elihu the Elephant
Emil the Eagle
Fantanimals
Freddy the Frog
Gloomy Gus the Hippopotamus
Here Come the Clowns

I Can Cook Cookbook
Ideals for Kids
In the Land of Sniggl-dee-Bloop
Little Sleepyheads
My Best Friend Ever
Read Aloud Stories
Ulysses S. Ant and Robert E. Flea
What If . . .
Ziggy and His Friends

Traditional favorites:

Amanda's Tree
Big Bunny Family Album
Bunny Tales
Cat Tales Family Album
A Christmas Carol
Christmas for Children
Dog Days Family Album
Favorite Christmas Carols

Jolly Old Santa Claus
The Night Before Christmas
Once Upon a Rhyme
Santa's Fun Book
The Story of Christmas for Children
The Story of Easter for Children
The Toy Shop Secret

0-89542-934-9 19

EXPLORING FOSSILS:
An Activity Book